THIS WALKER BOOK BELONGS TO:

_____

_____

_____

Janet Pedersen

Millie in the Meadow

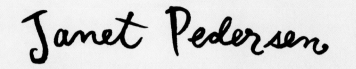

WALKER BOOKS
AND SUBSIDIARIES
LONDON · BOSTON · SYDNEY · AUCKLAND

Millie was happy in the meadow.
She had plenty of grass to munch
and lots of flowers to smell.
Best of all, Millie was
surrounded by her many
colourful friends.

One day, an artist came to the meadow.

Millie watched as he squeezed out bright, cheerful colours.

Maybe he will paint a picture of me! Millie thought.

First, the artist painted someone
with a small, red body
and black spots.

That's not me, Millie thought.

Millie swished her tail
and guessed.

Mooooo!
Must be Ladybird!

Next, the artist painted someone
with a round, purple body and
1, 2, 3, 4, 5, 6, 7, 8 skinny legs.

That's not me, Millie thought.

Millie swished her tail
and guessed.

Mooooo!
Must be Spider!

Then, the artist painted someone
with two tall ears and
a fluffy white tail.

That's not me, thought Millie.

Millie swished her tail
and guessed.

Mooooo!
Must be Bunny!

The artist kept painting while Millie
munched the grass, smelled the flowers
and played with her friends in the sunny
meadow. When the artist had finished,
he turned his painting round for Millie to see.

Millie recognized her friends
Ladybird, Spider and Bunny. And
right in the middle of the painting
was someone else — someone with
a white body and brown spots,
four legs and a long tail.

Millie thought this someone looked
very happy — as happy as she was.

Millie swished her tail and guessed...

For Graham

First published 2003 by Walker Books Ltd
87 Vauxhall Walk, London SE11 5HJ

This edition published 2004

2 4 6 8 10 9 7 5 3 1

© 2003 Janet Pedersen

The right of Janet Pedersen to be identified as author/illustrator
of this work has been asserted by her in accordance with
the Copyright, Designs and Patents Act 1988

This book has been typeset in Gararond Medium

Printed in China

British Library Cataloguing in Publication Data:
a catalogue record for this book
is available from the British Library

ISBN 1-84428-455-7

www.walkerbooks.co.uk

WALKER BOOKS is the world's leading independent
publisher of children's books. Working with
the best authors and illustrators we create books
for all ages, from babies to teenagers – books your child
will grow up with and always remember. So…

FOR THE BEST CHILDREN'S BOOKS, LOOK FOR THE BEAR